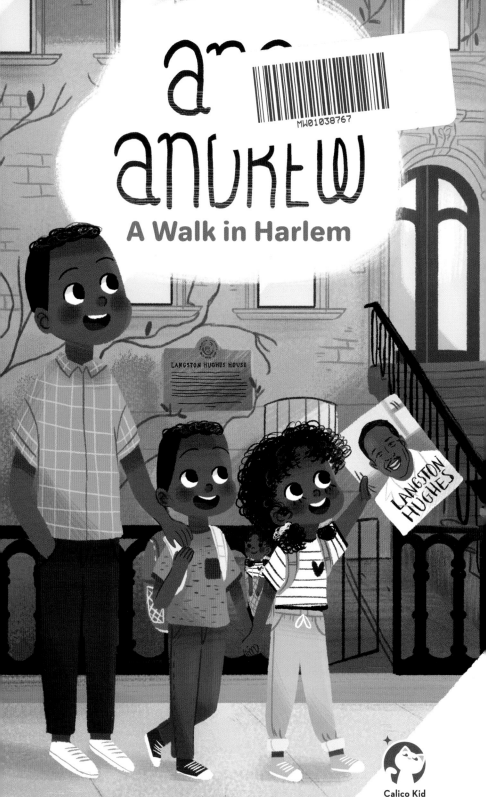

Ana & Andrew
A Walk in Harlem

LANGSTON HUGHES HOUSE

LANGSTON HUGHES

by Christine Platt
illustrated by Anuki López

Calico Kid
An Imprint of Magic Wagon
abdobooks.com

About the Author
Christine A. Platt is an author and scholar of African and African-American history. A beloved storyteller of the African diaspora, Christine enjoys writing historical fiction and non-fiction for people of all ages. You can learn more about her and her work at christineaplatt.com.

For every child, parent, caregiver and educator.
Thank you for reading Ana & Andrew! —CP

To Tanuki, my guardian angel with paws. —AL

abdobooks.com

Published by Magic Wagon, a division of ABDO, PO Box 398166, Minneapolis, Minnesota 55439. Copyright © 2021 by Abdo Consulting Group, Inc. International copyrights reserved in all countries. No part of this book may be reproduced in any form without written permission from the publisher. Calico Kid™ is a trademark and logo of Magic Wagon.

Printed in the United States of America, North Mankato, Minnesota.
102020
012021

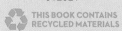

THIS BOOK CONTAINS
RECYCLED MATERIALS

Written by Christine Platt
Illustrated by Anuki López
Edited by Tyler Gieseke
Art Directed by Candice Keimig

Library of Congress Control Number: 2020941613

Publisher's Cataloging-in-Publication Data

Names: Platt, Christine, author. | López, Anuki, illustrator.
Title: A walk in Harlem / by Christine Platt ; illustrated by Anuki López.
Description: Minneapolis, Minnesota : Magic Wagon, 2021. | Series: Ana & Andrew
Summary: Papa surprises Ana & Andrew with a day trip to Harlem in New York City, where they learn about artists from the Harlem Renaissance. Later, they make their own art.
Identifiers: ISBN 9781532139710 (lib. bdg.) | ISBN 9781644945254 (pbk.) | ISBN 9781532139994 (ebook) | ISBN 9781098230135 (Read-to-Me ebook)
Subjects: LCSH: African American families--Juvenile fiction. | Travel--Juvenile fiction. | Museums--Juvenile fiction. | African American artists--Juvenile fiction. | Harlem Renaissance--Juvenile fiction. | Handicraft for children--Juvenile fiction.
Classification: DDC [E]--dc23

Table of Contents

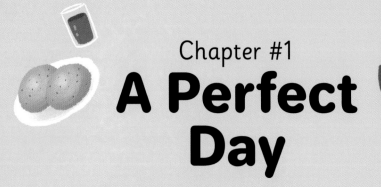

Chapter #1
A Perfect Day

It was a beautiful summer day. Ana and Andrew enjoyed playing outside in their backyard. Soon, it was time to go inside and get ready for dinner.

Mama cooked coconut bake, one of Andrew's favorites. The flat, round, and sweet bread was popular on the island of Trinidad, where Mama lived as a child.

Mama also made one of Ana's favorite dishes, macaroni and cheese.

Andrew stretched and patted his tummy. "Today was perfect. I can't think of a single thing that could make this day better."

Ana laughed. "Me and Sissy can't either!"

"I can!" Papa smiled. "Let's help Mama clear the dinner table, then I'll tell you."

Ana and Andrew loved surprises. And they couldn't imagine what could make their perfect day better.

As soon as they finished cleaning up, Ana asked, "What is it, Papa?"

Papa pulled two envelopes out of his pocket. He handed one to Ana and the other to Andrew. "Open them together. On the count of three."

"One . . . two . . . three!" When Ana and Andrew opened their envelopes, there were train tickets inside.

"Tomorrow, we are going to catch the train to New York City!" Papa exclaimed.

Ana twirled around excitedly with Sissy.

"Oh boy!" Andrew did a wiggle dance.

Mama laughed. "Baby Aaron and I are going to stay home. So, make sure to bring us back something special."

"We will!" Ana and Andrew said.

And Papa was right—getting train tickets to travel to New York made Ana and Andrew's day even more perfect.

Chapter #2
All Aboard!

Ana and Andrew woke up early the next morning. They were going to spend the day in New York! Papa told them they were going to visit an important neighborhood called Harlem.

Ana and Andrew wanted to have everything they would need in their backpacks.

"Make sure to pack notebooks and pencil cases," Papa reminded them. "You might be inspired by the things you see."

Papa, Ana, and Andrew gave Mama and baby Aaron lots of hugs and kisses goodbye. Then, they headed for the train station.

Ana and Andrew often rode on a special train called the Metro. It went to different places throughout Washington, DC, where they lived. But to travel to New York, they would ride a different train.

"Wow!" Ana admired the large train station made of white marble.

"This is Union Station," Papa said.
"And the station we're going to in
New York is called Penn Station."

Ana and Andrew waited in line with Papa. Soon, one of the train conductors called out, "All aboard!"

"Let's go!" Andrew said enthusiastically.

After handing their tickets to the conductor, Ana, Andrew, and Papa went through a special doorway.

When Ana and Andrew were in the train, they squealed. It was much bigger than the Metro. They took their seats as the train's whistle announced it was time to leave.

Ana held up Sissy so she could look out of the window too. "Off we go!"

Chapter #3
Hello, Harlem

The train ride from DC's Union Station to New York's Penn Station took almost four hours. Papa showed them all the states they passed through on a map.

When they finally arrived, Ana and Andrew couldn't believe how busy New York City was. It was even busier than DC!

"Get your New York slice!" a man called out from a pizza parlor.

"Papa, can we please have a slice of pizza?" Ana and Andrew asked.

"Of course!" Papa said. "Three slices please!"

Ana and Andrew bit into their large slices of pizza. "Delicious!"

When they finished eating, Papa hailed a yellow taxicab. "Can you please take us to Harlem?"

"You got it!" the taxi driver hollered.

"Why is Harlem so important?" Andrew asked.

"Is it next to Broadway, where the musicals are?" Ana wanted to know.

Papa laughed. "Harlem is not next to Broadway. But there was a time when Harlem was filled with its own music and musicals. In fact, that's what makes it so important."

Ana and Andrew listened closely.
"It was called the Harlem
Renaissance," Papa shared. "About
100 years ago, Harlem was a special
place for African American history
and culture."

"I know what history is," Andrew
said. "But what is culture?"

"Culture is a way of life," Papa explained. "It includes things like art, music, and books. During the Harlem Renaissance, many African Americans created important aspects of our culture. I'll show you where some of them lived!"

In Harlem, Papa held Ana and Andrew's hands as they walked around. First, he told them about a famous black painter named Jacob Lawrence. He grew up in Harlem.

Papa showed them one of Jacob's paintings on his phone. "Beautiful!" Ana and Andrew said.

"Some African Americans created music and plays," Papa told them as they walked. "Louis Armstrong, Duke Ellington, and Josephine Baker were a few."

Then, Papa stopped and pointed to a building that looked like a movie theater. "Some of them played right here, at the world-famous Apollo Theater!"

APOLLO

WELCOME to the WORLD FAMOUS
APOLLO THEATER

Their walk in Harlem ended in front of a large townhouse. "Many people wrote plays and books during the Harlem Renaissance too. A very famous poet named Langston Hughes lived right here!"

Ana and Andrew sat on the steps of Langston Hughes's former home and took lots of notes. They couldn't believe they were right where the Harlem Renaissance happened.

Chapter #4
Special Surprises

Soon, the sun was setting. It was time to catch a taxicab back to Penn Station.

"Can we please get more pizza?" Andrew asked. "New York pizza is soooooo good!"

Ana laughed. "Me and Sissy want more pizza too!"

"I do too!" Papa smiled.

Once they boarded the train back to DC, Ana and Andrew pulled out their notebooks and pencil cases. They'd definitely been inspired by Harlem. And they'd already decided on their special surprises for Mama and Aaron.

"No peeking, Papa!" Ana said. "It's a surprise for you too!"

Ana and Andrew worked on their special surprises during the entire train ride home.

"How was your trip to New York?" Mama asked when they came in the front door.

LANGSTON HUGHES

"Amazing!" Andrew said. "We learned all about the Harlem Renaissance."

"And we ate some really delicious pizza." Ana giggled.

"Harlem inspired Ana and Andrew," Papa said. "They have special surprises for us."

APOLLO
WELCOME to the WORLD FAMOUS
APOLLO THEATER

"That's right!" Ana and Andrew pulled out their notebooks.

"Oh my!" Mama said excitedly. Aaron burped, and everyone laughed.

"Here's mine!" Ana held up her notebook. It was a drawing inspired by the Jacob Lawrence painting Papa had shown them.

"Beautiful!" Mama exclaimed.

"And I wrote my first poem," Andrew said proudly.

"Congratulations," Papa said. "We can't wait to hear it!"

Andrew read from his notebook:

A walk in Harlem on a sunny day.

We learned where people once loved to play.

They made art and music. Some sang the blues.

A walk in Harlem on a sunny day.

We learned where people once loved to play.

They made art and music. Some sang the blues.

Some people wrote poetry. And I did too!

Some people wrote poetry. And I did too!

Everyone clapped happily. Even Aaron clapped! Ana and Andrew smiled. They were proud to celebrate the Harlem Renaissance.